George and the Baby

by Althea
illustrated by the author

Published by Rourke Enterprises, Inc., P.O. Box 929, Windermere, Florida 32786. Copyright © 1981 by Rourke Enterprises, Inc. All copyrights reserved. No part of this book may be reproduced in any form without written permission from the publisher. Printed in the United States of America.

Library of Congress Cataloging in Publication Data

Althea.
  George and the baby.

  Summary: George the dachshund feels left out when his master and mistress bring a new baby home.
  [1. Dogs—Fiction. 2. Babies—Fiction]
I. Title.
PZ7.A4638Ge 1981   [E]   81-13757
ISBN 0-86592-564-X   AACR2

Rourke Enterprises, Inc.
Windermere, Florida 32786

I am a Dachshund.
My name is George.
We live in the country,
where there are lots of trees.

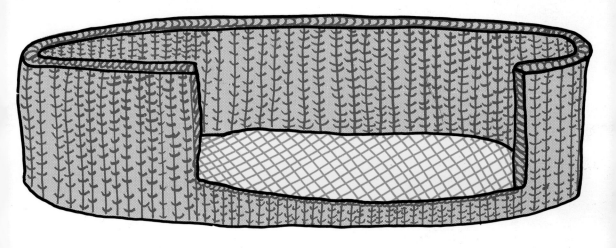

I have a comfortable bed in the kitchen.
My master and mistress are very kind to me.

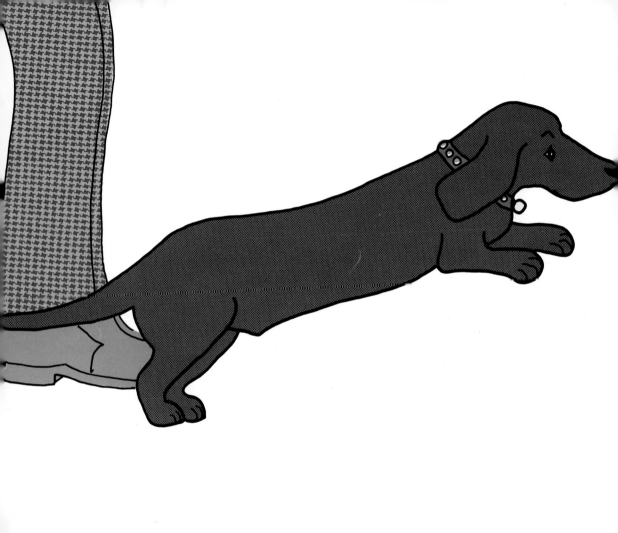

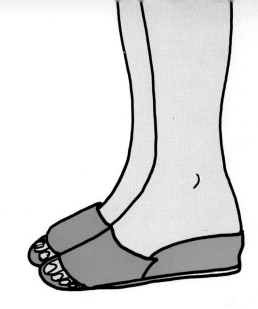

They always play games with me
and we all love each other.

When their friends
come to the house
they pat me,
and make a fuss over me.

But one day my mistress came home
with something new.

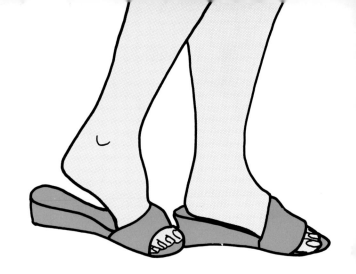

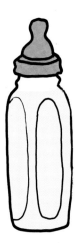

She called him a *baby*.
Everyone gave him
a lot of attention.

My mistress was always making him
nice things to eat and drink.

She pushed him in his baby carriage.
We did not play in the woods anymore.
I had to wear my leash all the time.

"What a lovely
baby!"
"—Ooh,
he is sweet!"

When their friends visited
they played with the baby.

No one played with me any more.
I was very unhappy.

Unified School District No. 317
Herndon, Kansas 67739

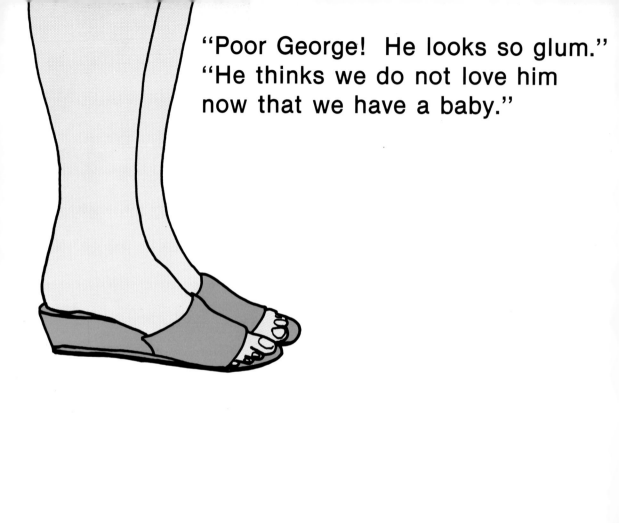

"Poor George! He looks so glum."
"He thinks we do not love him
now that we have a baby."

"Silly George! Of course we still love him."
"We love George and the baby."

I listened carefully.
"So they love *both* of us," I thought.

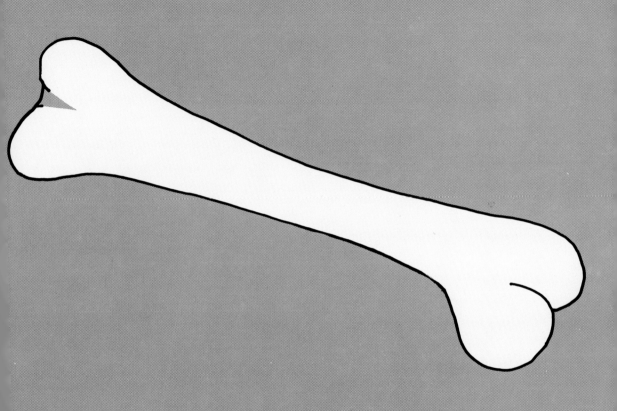

They gave me an extra large bone that day.

They showed me the baby.
He was very small.

They said I could
sit by the baby
carriage and look
after him. He
was really very nice.

The baby has grown bigger now.

We often play games together.

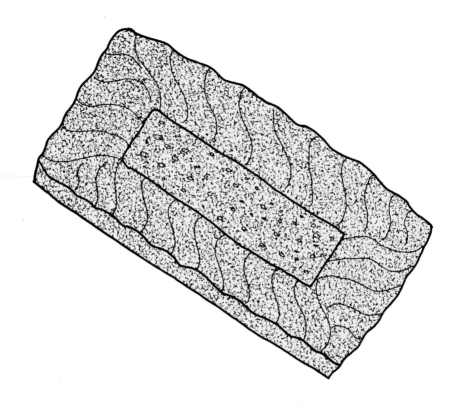

He sometimes gives me some of his cookies.

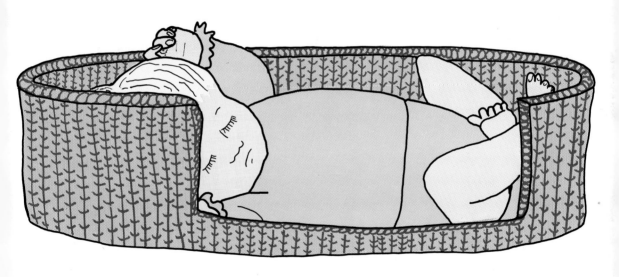

One day I will let him sleep in my basket.

Everyone says I am a great help
looking after him.

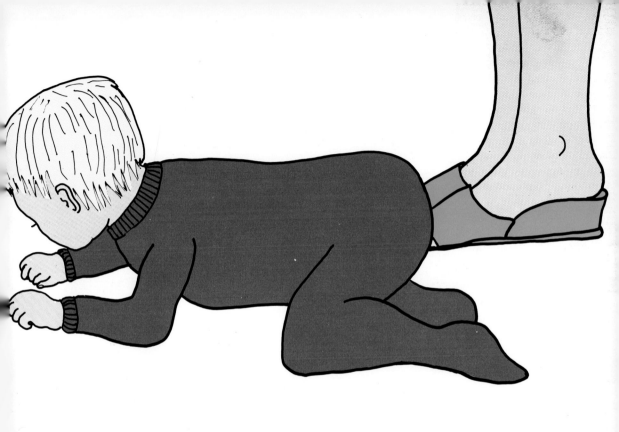

We *all* love each other.